3. A Race Against Time

Everybody in the team had scored at least twice, with Ryan claiming a personal tally of ten! By their own reckoning, they seemed to have scored three more than the official total given to them by the umpires, but they were not complaining. Rangers still ran out winners 33–27.

The last word was left to Stopper. He hammered the ball home from the halfway line with stunning power, giving Sasha no hope of keeping it out.

"What a shot!" gasped Vicki as they shook hands afterwards.

Stopper grinned at her. "Yeah, not bad, eh, for a great-great-great-grandad!"

TIME RANGERS

3. A Race Against Time

Rob Childs

Hippo

DAZZA
GOAL KEEPER — 1

WORM
RIGHT-BACK — 2

STOPPER
CENTRE-BACK — 5

RAKESH
RIGHT-MIDFIELD — 4

MR. STOPPARD
MANAGER

JACKO
CENTRE-MIDFIELD — 8

SPEEDIE
RIGHT-WINGER — 7

RYAN
CENTRE-FORWARD — 9

ANIL
LEFT-WINGER — 11

MR. THOMAS
MANAGER

For my wife Joy, with special thanks

Scholastic Children's Books,
Commonwealth House, 1–19 New Oxford Street,
London WC1A 1NU, UK
a division of Scholastic Ltd
London ~ New York ~ Toronto ~ Sydney ~ Auckland

Published in the UK by Scholastic Ltd, 1997

ISBN 0 590 19118 7

Typeset by DP Photosetting, Aylesbury, Bucks.
Printed by Cox & Wyman Ltd, Reading, Berks.

10 8 6 4 2 1 3 5 7 9

1 Seven Souls

"Goal!" cried Ryan. "Unstoppable!"

Dazza picked himself up out of a soggy tussock of long grass. "Huh! Wouldn't have gone in if we had proper posts."

The keeper gave his massive goalposts a hard stare. They towered above him, misshapen and pockmarked, and he might have kicked out at them in disgust, if they hadn't been made of solid rock.

The prehistoric stone circle had no doubt witnessed many strange sights over the centuries, but perhaps nothing quite like Ryan's sliced volley. The ball struck one of the seven great slabs of gritstone and looped behind the beaten Dazza in a slow, graceful arc to clip its neighbour. This was leaning back at an angle of about sixty degrees and deflected the ball inwards for a goal.

"That was my special trick shot," Ryan grinned.

Dazza slapped the snow off his tracksuit. "Still reckon the stones round the other side of the circle are better than these," he grumbled.

"Just 'cos they're closer together!" laughed Jacko.

After the overnight snowfall, the organizers of Tanfield Rangers under-12s' soccer tour of the Peak District had declared Wednesday a "rest" day. The players were delighted that the planned hill walk was now cancelled, but they were not going to let a bit of snow stop them from having a game of football. Straight after breakfast, captain Jacko had led most of the squad through the slushy field next to the moorland campsite for an energetic kickabout.

Michael Winter, better known as Worm, was not among them. He'd got up early to explore the ancient monument all by himself without being disturbed. He wanted to soak up the atmosphere of the site in the eerie, white stillness of the dawn.

Worm was a good defender for the Rangers, but he preferred history to football. He read, ate and dreamt it. And this week, following each of their first two matches, he'd even been living it. For him and several of his teammates, the Easter tour had involved rather more travelling than they'd ever expected. Travelling back through time!

"Where's Worm gone?" asked Stopper.

"He's mooched off to those old burial mounds over there," said Jacko.

Keith Stoppard looked across the field.

"Oh yeah, I can see him. He's standing right up on top of the biggest one."

"Probably wishing he was there when they were actually being made," put in Ryan, not trying too hard to disguise a sneer in his voice.

Jacko winced. "We'll have to make sure he doesn't go dragging us back with him to prehistoric times. That'd really be going too far."

"You can say that again!" hooted Dazza, belting the ball away for the players to chase once more.

Jacko smiled ruefully. "You know what I mean. It's just that I'm beginning to think all this crazy time-warp business must have something to do with Worm."

"How do you work that out?" said the keeper.

"Well, have you realized it's always Worm who disappears first? He seems to trigger things off somehow."

"Come on, Worm's not exactly Doctor Who!" scoffed Stopper.

The captain shrugged. "Don't ask me how it happens. I guess even he doesn't know, but it's a pretty weird coincidence, eh?"

"Worm's pretty weird to start off with," said Ryan uncharitably.

There was no chance for any further debate. The ball flew across the goalmouth again and the four of them were swallowed back up into the hectic,

kick-and-rush action around the giant standing stones. Both sides were shooting into the same goal and mistakes were costly. Any stray pass or shot might easily result in the other team scoring instead.

That happened now. Rakesh on the right dribbled skilfully through the melting snow and tried to find Stopper with his centre. Ryan was goal-hanging as usual, lurking behind Stopper, and darted past him to make first contact with the ball. His touch was firm and accurate, but Dazza was alert to the danger and made a smart save.

The footballers were so involved in their free-for-all that they failed to notice Worm sidle up through the circle a few minutes later – until he spoke. "Enjoying yourselves?"

Ryan and Stopper had just wrestled each other to the ground in trying to win a loose ball and now scrambled back to their feet.

"Sure are," Ryan gasped. "What's up with you? You look like you've swallowed a mouthful of vinegar."

"He doesn't approve of us doing this," Stopper said.

"Doing what?"

"Playing football here."

"We're not doing any harm," said Ryan defiantly as he turned on Worm. "We're not vandals, you know. We're not scratching the score on the stones or anything."

"I just think we should treat the site with a bit more respect, that's all," Worm said. "This circle's about four thousand years old."

"That makes it just lumps of old rock, then," Ryan growled. "What's so precious about it?"

"Lots of things. Might have been a place of worship once, like a kind of temple. They might even have had human sacrifices here to please the gods."

That last piece of speculation was meant to capture Ryan's imagination. And it succeeded. "Who might?" demanded the striker.

"Oh, Druids, maybe."

Ryan gave a low whistle and looked at the circle in a new light. "Hey! Hear that, lads? Worm reckons the old Druids cut people's heads off at this place."

"I didn't say that," Worm sighed, but it was too late. The other players were already wandering up in the hope of more gory details. Worm found himself suddenly with an audience.

"Do any of you know what this ancient circle is actually called?" he asked them.

There was much shaking of heads. "Ye Olde Wembley Stadium?" Rakesh suggested to set them giggling.

"The *Seven Souls*," Worm announced.

"How do you know that?" said Jacko.

"I've been to the campsite office. They've got a leaflet there about it. Makes very interesting reading."

"This sounds like it could be a long story," groaned Ryan, slumping against one of the stones to affect boredom.

"It's been given that name for a good reason," Worm continued.

"I expect it has," said Dazza wearily. "C'mon, tell us, and then perhaps we can get on with our game again."

"Because it's haunted..."

2 Day trip

"Not so sure I want to go too near that circle now," admitted Dazza. "At least not on my own."

"Nor me," agreed Rakesh. "Bet it'd feel dead spooky."

The footballers were back in the campsite, but Worm's ghost stories still preyed on their minds. The tales told of glowing stones and shadowy figures flitting about the circle in the moonlight. There were always seven, one for each of the stones . . .

"You don't believe all that guff, do you?" Ryan scoffed.

Dazza scratched his head. "The way this week is working out, I think I might believe anything."

"C'mon, you lot, gather round," cried Mr Thomas, one of the Rangers' two managers. "We're setting off soon."

"Setting off, Dad?" echoed Ryan. "Thought you said it'd be too risky to go up on the hills today."

"It is. So we've decided to take you all on a magical mystery tour!"

"Hey, brill! Where to?"

"If we told you that, it wouldn't be much of a mystery, would it?"

His co-manager, Mr Stoppard, appeared with a camera. "I come from round here originally, remember," he said. "Still got family in the area. I'm going to show you some of my boyhood haunts."

"Wish your dad hadn't used that last word!" Rakesh whispered to Stopper out of the corner of his mouth.

"We want to take a group photo first to prove to people back home it really snowed here this Easter," said Mr Stoppard. "Perhaps some of you could have snowballs in your hands..."

That was asking for it. Dutifully, several players bent down to scoop up some snow – and then threw it at the managers, giving them no time for evasive action. Soon a full-blooded snowball fight was under way, the boys dodging among the tents for cover as the missiles whistled through the air.

"Got you smack on the head, Dad!" Stopper cackled.

"I'll get even, don't worry," came the promise as order was restored and the players regrouped for the photograph. There were more positional changes than in the whole of the past season, but finally Mr Stoppard was satisfied. "Smile!"

"GOAL!" they all cheered as the shutter clicked.

"Right, we hit the road in ten minutes," announced Mr Thomas. "Make sure you've got your coats and wellies – and swimming trunks."

"Cossies?" gasped Jacko in delight. "That must be the magical bit!"

"Just a minute, Worm, er, I mean, Michael," said Mr Stoppard as the players ran to fetch their gear from the tents. "Could I ask you to do me a favour? Take a snap of Keith and me for the family album, like."

"Sure," Worm agreed. "Where do you want it?"

Mr Stoppard stood with his arm proudly round his son's shoulders next to one of the two hired minibuses as Worm fiddled about with the camera. He was trying to capture the stone circle in the background too.

"Ready?" he asked, finger poised over the button. "OK, got it!"

"Lovely, thanks," said the manager, and then shoved a huge handful of snow right down the back of Stopper's shirt!

"Right, first stop, everybody out!" called the driver.

"Where are we?" piped up Anil, the Rangers' gangling winger, as the boys tumbled out of the back of the buses.

"Grangelow," said Mr Stoppard. "I want to show Keith the village where his old dad was born."

"Fascinating," muttered Ryan under his breath.

"Is this where we go swimming?" asked Jacko hopefully.

"'Fraid not," Mr Stoppard smiled. "The water here is for drinking."

The party was soon standing in front of a large, sprawling tree, whose maze of branches were on the point of bursting into leaf. Nearby, a spring of clear water bubbled out from a stone arch to pour into a shallow pool and then run away into a culvert.

"Ah, grand to see the well and the Victoria Oak again," Mr Stoppard sighed. "I used to climb this tree when I was a young boy, you know."

"Bet you can't do it now, Dad."

"Cheeky monkey!" he chuckled, resisting the temptation to have a go. "Wouldn't want to risk damaging it. This oak tree was planted way back in the early nineteenth century to mark the coronation of Queen Victoria. And no, before you ask, I wasn't around to see it!"

Stopper grinned. "I thought Auntie Vicky was pulling my leg when she once told me she was named after a tree. Is this the one?"

"Indeed it is. Looks good for a few hundred years yet, I hope."

His dad's nostalgia, like the spring, was in full flow. "I remember us doing a well-dressing for the Oak Tree Well as kids."

"What's a well-dressing?" asked Worm out of genuine interest.

"Surprised a lad like you hasn't heard of this ancient custom. Goes right back to pagan times."

"Like when people worshipped water spirits and that?" said Worm.

"You've got it. Only now it's a form of thanksgiving ceremony – and a tourist attraction, of course!"

Some of the footballers began to fidget and Mr Thomas looked at his watch. His fellow manager, however, continued his explanation. "Every year many Peakland villages decorate their wells with huge mosaic pictures, all done in flower petals mostly. They're amazingly beautiful..."

He seemed lost in memories for a moment and then spoke again. "Ours was the Victoria Oak. I can still see it now. Its title was: 'Trees help the planet to breathe'."

Mr Thomas started to usher the restless boys back to the buses and tugged Worm away as well, leaving Stopper alone with his dad.

"Sorry I can't show you around the village a bit more, Keith."

"Another time, Dad, eh? Guess I'll have to come back here again in the future."

It was a good day out.

After leaving Grangelow, the boys

went on to enjoy a tour of the caves at
Castleton and explored the castle ruins
overlooking the town. Fun and games in
a Sheffield swimming pool helped to cool
everyone off and now, late in the evening, they were warming themselves up
again. As the buses chugged their way
across the moonlit moors back to the
campsite, the passengers were tucking
into bags of steaming fish and chips.

"Don't look so disappointed, Worm,"

Rakesh said, slurping on a hot, greasy chip. "I mean, you can't expect to go time-travelling every day."

Ryan gave a loud snort. "Huh! Seems like it this week!"

"I really felt something was going to happen at that castle," Worm sighed, shaking his head sadly. "It just seemed such a perfect situation – and yet..."

"Reckon we got off lightly," mumbled Dazza through a mouthful of cod. "Every time we went through an archway, I thought we were gonna bump into some medieval knight or peasant."

"Yeah, I noticed we all steered well clear of Worm," laughed Anil.

"I try and do that anyway," Ryan sniggered.

"I think we're getting a touch of Wormophobia," Jacko decided. "A fear of finding ourselves too near Worm and in danger of being whisked away into another time!"

The Rangers soon broke into a series of raucous football chants, making Mr Thomas suffer a very noisy end to the journey. As he turned into the site, the headlight beams swept across the field.

"Hello, there's some people at that old circle," he remarked. "You wouldn't catch me round there in the dark. Place gives me the creeps."

The boys had glimpsed the figures, too, and fell strangely silent. As they sipped hot drinks before crawling into their two-berth tents, they cast nervous glances towards the stones, silhouetted in the moonlight.

"Perhaps the Druids are sacrificing someone for not doing their share of the washing-up," Ryan said to try and raise a cheap laugh.

He failed. Nobody thought it was very funny.

Sleep was a long time coming for most of the footballers. The wind seemed to be making more weird noises than necessary outside the thin, protective canvas of their tents.

Worm was still wide awake. "You asleep, Anil?" he whispered to his partner.

"Yes," came the muffled answer from deep inside the next sleeping bag.

"Thought you were. When you wake up, do you want to sneak across to the circle and have a look round?"

"In the morning, you mean?"

"No, now..."

"What!" Anil's head popped up out of the bag as though a catch had suddenly been released. "Have you gone mad?"

"Sshh! Not so loud. You always start shouting when you get excited."

"I'm not shouting!" Anil exclaimed loudly. "I am *not* going across there in the middle of the night. Got that, Worm? Repeat – no, not ever, not in a million years!"

Worm wasn't one to be put off easily once he'd got an idea in his head. "Do I take it, then, that you might possibly consider coming with me...?"

3 Spooky!

Two hunched figures scurried across the low wall behind the tents and into the field, jeans and jumpers pulled hastily over their pyjamas.

"I must be crazy, letting you talk me into doing this."

"Quiet!" Worm said, putting a finger to his lips. "Just follow me and keep your eyes peeled for any sign of life."

"What about any sign of death?" Anil grunted, and then wished he hadn't said that. He wished he wasn't here at all.

They crept up to a small mound near the *Seven Souls* circle and squatted down.

"Ugh! It's all wet!" Anil gasped in dismay.

"Will you shut up! Don't know why I asked you to come with me."

"'Cos you didn't dare come by yourself."

"Not that at all. I just wanted somebody else to back me up in the morning if we see anything. The others won't believe me."

"What are you expecting to see?"

"Dunno. Probably nothing."

"Let's hope so – then we can get back to our tent. I'm cold."

"Stop moaning," Worm told him with irritation and then immediately grabbed Anil's arm. "Look – there!"

Anil almost broke the school high jump record. "Where?" he hissed when he could hear himself speak above the thumping of his heart.

"False alarm, just a trick of the light. Thought I saw something move on the far side."

Anil swallowed great gulps of relief. "Don't *ever* do that again!"

"Sorry, guess I'm a bit jumpy myself," Worm apologized, rising slowly to his feet. "I'm going closer – want to make sure nobody's here."

Anil didn't fancy being left by himself and was forced to follow. "They might be hiding behind the stones," he said with a quaking voice.

"Doubt it. But if anything leaps out and grabs me, you leg it back to camp, right, and wake everybody up."

They reached the nearest stone, one of Dazza's goalposts, without mishap. Worm let the tension go out of his shoulders and his tight, shallow breathing became more regular. He leant his hand on to the stone for support and immediately snatched it back.

"What's the matter?"

"It's warm!" Worm exclaimed in utter amazement.

"Don't be daft, that's impossible. Not on a night like this."

"You feel it."

"No way."

"C'mon, Anil, please. Just to prove I'm not making it up."

Anil stepped tentatively forwards, holding out his hand at full stretch as if pretending it didn't belong to him. First his fingertips, and then his flat palm joined Worm's on the hard, rough surface.

"You're right, it *is* warm! How's it doing that?"

Worm shook his head, running his hand along the broad base where it felt even warmer, and then moving across the gap to touch the next stone. "This one's just the same. Doesn't make sense."

Anil's eyes grew wider than ever. "Look!" he gasped. "That stone over there, it's glowing..."

"And humming too," gulped Worm. "Listen!"

They listened – and then ran. Their nerve broke, and without any kind of signal, they both bolted away across the field, back towards the hoped-for safety of the campsite and their own little tent.

Worm lagged behind the faster Anil and stumbled when he kicked something lying in the long grass. If he didn't know any better, he'd have said it felt like a football...

"Look at them over there."

Ryan stood up, still eating his fried breakfast of bacon and eggs. He pointed to a group of youngsters about their own age who were kicking a ball around in the field. All the snow had now gone.

"Where did that lot spring from?" asked Dazza. "Didn't see any sign of them on the site yesterday."

"Must have arrived while we were out

and about," said Stopper. "It was dark when we got back, remember."

Everybody remembered only too well, even though Worm and Anil had not yet shared the secret of their nocturnal fright. They didn't want to risk ridicule.

"Weird kit they've got on," Jacko observed as the newcomers now became the centre of interest. "Anybody recognize the clubs they support?"

"Hard to keep track, the way most of 'em keep changing their strips so often," said Dazza. "Must be some yukky, away-kit colours."

"Like to get a closer look," Jacko said. "See whose names they've got on their backs, then we'll know."

"Let's go and thrash 'em," Ryan grinned. "Show 'em how good the Rangers are."

"There's only seven of them," said Anil. "And two are girls!"

"So? We'll play seven-a-side," said Ryan, unwilling to listen to any objections. "Who wants a game of footie after breakfast?"

Most of the hands went up, but not Worm's. He intended to go back and have a good scout around that circle. He was determined to try and get to the bottom of the mystery of the glowing stones.

"Nobody goes anywhere until you've cleared up all this mess and tidied your tents," Mr Stoppard cut in. "Chores first, then play."

"No shirking your duties," said Mr Thomas. "Especially you, Ryan!"

"That's not fair, picking on me, Dad."

"Yes it is. I know what a litterbug you are. Your bedroom at home is like a rubbish dump."

Grumbling, Ryan went back to the tent he shared with Jacko. In defiance, he picked up an empty drinks can discarded inside the tent flap and tossed it into the hedge behind.

"Right, that's one dealt with," he muttered, satisfied with his little victory over his dad. He also hoped Jacko wouldn't discover the crumpled crisps packet he stuffed inside his partner's sleeping bag.

The Rangers found the other children enjoying the sunshine, their ball abandoned. Ryan picked it up.

"This ball's a bit light," he called out to them. "Feels funny. What's it made of?"

"Oh, nothing special," came the casual reply from one of the boys.

"We've got a proper leather ball," Ryan told him. "Fancy a game?"

"Love to," a dark-haired girl laughed. "We hoped you might have time to play."

Dazza grinned. "Time's one thing we seem to have lots of this week."

"We're on a soccer tour," Jacko explained. "You guys on holiday?"

"Let's call it a flying visit," another boy grinned, introducing himself as Tony. "Just to see what it's like here."

Some of the names on their shirts appeared as they stood up.

"Wren, Bannister, Zannini, Julio," Stopper read out one by one. "Never heard of these players."

The children exchanged quick glances.

"Um, well, you'll have to try and remember them," answered the blonde girl hesitantly. "They're up and coming stars of the future. Maybe you haven't seen them play yet."

"Hey! That's a United shirt you've got on, isn't it?" Ryan realized. "They're my favourite team. Didn't know they'd changed their sponsors for next season."

As she turned round, all the Rangers burst out laughing – except Ryan. He was too stunned. He found himself

staring at a large number nine on the back of her blue shirt, the number he always wore. And also at his own name in white capital letters – THOMAS.

4 Out of place

The newcomers' enthusiasm and soccer ability were not matched, it seemed, by their knowledge of the game's rules.

"Handball!" cried Rakesh.

"Remember you're not allowed to catch the ball, Vicki," said one of her teammates. "That's twice you've done it already."

"Probably thinks she's playing netball," Anil giggled.

"Let her off," cut in Ryan. "She's only a girl."

Vicki glared at him. "What's *that* supposed to mean?" she demanded.

"Who do you think you are to say that?"

"Ryan Thomas! And you've got my shirt on!" he retorted, making her bite her lip. "I'm gonna play for United one day, you mark my words."

"Hmm ... I think you probably will," she said quietly to herself.

There were enough players for almost a full-side game, with Vicki's group shared between the two teams. Vicki herself showed she could control the ball with her feet too. She took a pass in her stride and burst past a flimsy challenge from Anil to strike the ball only just wide of Dazza's goal. The shot brushed the pile of coats put down as posts.

"Hey, you *can* play!" said Ryan in admiration. "Sorry about what I said earlier."

She smiled. "Forget it. Just wish I could shoot like you. That goal of yours was tremendous."

"Yeah, but we're still losing. Pity Dazza's not on our side. He's the only decent keeper we've got."

"Why not let Sasha go in goal for us? She's superb there."

"She's on Jacko's team."

"Well, we can do a swap, can't we? Offer him an extra goal as well."

"Are you crazy? What kind of a deal is that?"

"I think you'll find it's a very good one."

There was something about the confident way Vicki spoke that prompted Ryan to propose the bizarre transfer.

"You want *both* the girls on your side now?" Jacko said in disbelief. "Now I've heard everything. You always make jokes at school when you see girls playing soccer in Games."

Ryan shrugged. "Some of them are OK," he said lamely.

Jacko wasn't going to argue, and Sasha immediately took up her position between the coats. "Ryan must have fallen in love," Stopper cackled. "Seeing his name on Vicki's shirt has gone to his head!"

The joke was soon on Jacko's team. The new goalkeeper was outstanding. Sasha was only beaten once in the rest of the game when a shot hit a bump and evaded her grasp.

It wasn't long before Ryan put his side ahead, but after Vicki slipped the ball past Dazza to make the score 7–4, she flopped down on to the grass. "Sorry,

Ryan, I'm done in now," she panted. "Need a rest."

It was the signal for all her friends to drop out of the game, too. They went to sit nearby to soak up more of the spring sunshine, leaving the Rangers to continue playing until they took a breather themselves.

"Weird lot," murmured Jacko. "Can't quite suss them out."

Ryan agreed. "They keep coming out with dead stupid things. That Tony asked me why sheep were left outside overnight, and what's it like playing football in the rain. And as for their kit!"

"They almost seem out of place, somehow," Jacko mused aloud. "You know, as if they don't really belong here..."

"I don't reckon they do." It was Worm's voice, right behind them. "Found this metal box hidden near one of the stones. I think it's some kind of fancy, electronic control unit."

"Like for those remote-control planes and things?" Ryan said.

There was a distinct gleam in Worm's eyes. "A bit more sophisticated than that. It might even be your new pals' means of transport."

"What are you getting at, Worm?" Jacko said, beginning to lose his patience. "C'mon, spit it out."

"OK, then. What I'm holding, I believe, is a time machine!"

"This thing yours, by any chance?"

Worm produced the shiny box from behind his back and the visitors gasped. "Where did you find that?" demanded Tony in alarm.

"Where you left it," Worm smirked. "You should take more care of something like this – in future..."

"There's a time-factor at work here, isn't there?" said Jacko, more as a statement of fact than a question. "I can sense it."

The other children had no opportunity to try and deny it as Worm explained what he and Anil had seen during the night. "I started to put two and two together – and got seven as the answer."

"Seven?" queried Dazza. "And I thought my maths was bad!"

"Seven stones, seven mysterious newcomers, seven red buttons on here," said Worm. "I don't believe in ghosts – but I *do* believe in time travel!"

"We've, er, had some experience of it ourselves this week," Jacko put in to back Worm up.

"So what time do you people come from?" Worm persisted.

They were clearly shocked to have been discovered, but Vicki at least was prepared to own up to the truth. "2151," she answered boldly.

Anil scratched his head. "Nine minutes to ten at night?"

"She's not talking about the twenty-four-hour clock, stupid," Ryan jibed at him. "She means the *year* 2151!"

"How many of you are travellers?" Tony asked.

Jacko didn't need to count. "Just us seven," he replied. "We sent the others back to camp. They know nothing about our adventures."

"Best to keep us a secret too, if you can," said Tony. "But now we must return. Our time-permit here has nearly run out."

They walked over towards the circle together. "May we have our T.A.C. back, please?" asked Vicki.

"T.A.C.?" Worm repeated, reluctantly handing over the small box he was still nursing.

"Time Activator Control," she explained. "I hope you've not been tampering with it."

"I was tempted," he grinned. "Tell me,

what were you doing here last night?"

"That was a test run," she replied, adjusting some of the dials on the control unit. "The system isn't free of gremlins yet."

"You mean, it's not guaranteed you'll get back safely?"

"Oh, yes, that's no problem. We can set the exact time co-ordinates. It's the travelling backwards that's not quite so accurate. We arrived during the night by mistake and it was too cold to stay."

"Why did you decide to come here?"

"To play football!"

"What?" Worm gasped. "You could have done that in your own garden."

Vicki shook her head. "We don't have gardens. And the air isn't clean enough to go running about outside playing games. Things have changed in the future, I'm afraid."

"Not for the better, by the sound of it," said Worm, appalled.

"It's not as bad as it might have been," she replied vaguely, then suddenly made him an amazing offer. "You can take a look at what it's like for yourselves, if you wish. We're allowed to invite time-guests for a short stay."

Worm's whole face lit up. "You really mean that? Wow! 2151…"

He stopped as the date stirred something in his memory. "Hey! That's exactly two hundred years since the Park was set up, isn't it? Back in 1951, the Peak District was the first of the National Parks."

Vicki was impressed. "That's right. Time travel seems to work best when it homes in on anniversaries – and even on links between people. We got a very high link-reading on our scales this trip for some reason."

Worm was too excited to start wondering why that was. But when he gabbled out the great news to his teammates, they did not share his enthusiasm.

"Hold on," said Ryan. "*You* might want to go flying off into the unknown, but I don't."

"Let's put it to the vote," Worm pleaded. "C'mon, we can't miss a chance like this. All those who want to see the future, raise your hand."

Worm's own hand shot up as he spoke, followed more hesitantly by those of Dazza and Rakesh.

"There, outvoted," cried Ryan in

triumph.

"Just a minute, I'm still thinking about it," said Stopper. "Perhaps we could have a quick look at next Saturday on the way by."

"Why next Saturday?" asked Jacko, puzzled.

"Well, if we saw which six numbers came up on the National Lottery, when we got back I could tell Dad to buy a ticket!"

"I don't think time travel is meant to be used for that sort of thing," said Worm in disapproval.

"Pity. Anyway, I wouldn't mind getting an idea of the shape of things to come. Might be able to put the experience to some good use."

"Four-three to us," Worm gloated. "We win."

"It's all of us or none of us, I reckon," said Jacko. "I'm willing to risk it. What about you, Anil?"

"Guess so," sighed Anil in resignation. "What do we have to do?"

"Don't worry, they'll explain all that. They know what they're doing," Worm assured him. "Ryan?"

"OK," he shrugged, trying to act cool. "As long as I can take our football to play with."

"You know what happened to the others," Dazza warned him. "They didn't come back."

"I'll look after it," Ryan insisted, and then he went on the attack. "Hey, Tony! Since you future people are so clever, how come you couldn't get the players' names right on the shirts?"

Tony smiled. "Looks like my research into the old soccer records must have been too hasty before we left. I think I was possibly about ten years out. Maybe Thomas's time is yet to come..."

He slipped the others a wink as Ryan suddenly went very quiet, lost in thought.

5 Back to the future

"Each of you must stand with one of us in contact with a stone," Tony explained as they prepared to leave. The stones were already warm.

"Do we *have* to hold hands?" Stopper said to Vicki in dismay.

His partner smiled, enjoying the boy's embarrassment. "Either that or you can put both arms round me and cling on tight."

"I'll hold hands!" he decided, pulling a face.

Vicki laughed. "By the way, why do they call you Stopper?"

"Well, partly because they think I'm just a big, clumsy defender."

"And partly?" she prompted.

"Because my name's Keith Stoppard."

She nodded thoughtfully. "I thought it might be."

Before he could say anything in reply, Vicki pressed the green button on the control panel. "OK, everybody, take a deep breath. Away we go!"

The ancient stones glowed brighter, hummed and throbbed – and the few Rangers who still had their eyes open saw the field suddenly disappear. Even Worm closed his eyes then.

When he blinked them back open, only a second or two later, it seemed, he found himself inside a large domed room. His stomach felt like it hadn't yet arrived. Worm could see from the pained faces of his teammates nearby that they were suffering similar reactions.

"Time sickness," said Tony. "It's quite

common. You'll all need to take travel pills before we show you around outside."

The footballers gazed at their new surroundings in wonder. The curved walls were lined with unmanned banks of computer screens and rows of coloured, flashing lights.

"I've never seen anything like it," said Anil in a whisper.

"I have," said Rakesh. "But only on the flight deck of the Starship Enterprise."

"It all seems like science fiction to me," murmured Dazza.

"This is science fact," Sasha assured them. "Welcome to the future!"

"I can hardly believe it," breathed Jacko. "Only yesterday we were fighting in the Civil War, hundreds of years ago..."

"Day before that, actually," Worm corrected him gently.

The centre-piece of the room was the prehistoric circle, even though the stones now jutted out through the smooth, polished floor instead of the springy grass of the field. Some of the boys stayed in close touch with them to try and preserve their shaky sense of reality.

"Have these stones been moved somewhere else?" said Ryan accusingly.

"No, you're still standing on the same spot," Tony said. "This control centre has been built around them to harness the Earth's forces."

"Sort of like magnetic forces, you mean?" asked Worm.

"Something like that." Tony gave a slight shrug, uncertain himself exactly how the process of time travel worked. "The Earth's own energy forces are transmitted through these stones. Our chief dowsers have discovered how to collect this power and increase it."

"Dowsers?" repeated Worm in

astonishment. "I thought they went around with bits of twigs and metal rods finding out where water was."

"They can also detect lines of energy underground," Tony told him. "But locating water is still their most important work. It has to be. Good quality water is quite scarce."

"Think I could do with a drink now," Stopper admitted, feeling queasy. "Have you got some to spare?"

"Of course," said Vicki. "There's bottled water in the recovery room. Follow me, everyone, while my brother goes to arrange some transport."

"I didn't realize you and Tony were related," said Stopper as she came to sit next to him on one of the couches. "Funny, my dad's got a sister called Victoria, and so have I. The name kind of runs in our family."

"It still does," Vicki grinned at him.

"How do you mean?"

"You'll see," she said mysteriously. "Can't wait for our father to meet you later. He's the Director of this centre, you know."

"Oh, what's his name?"

"Professor Stoppard!"

Stopper dropped his bottle of water on to the floor.

The seven Rangers piled after Vicki and Tony into a long, sleek hoverbus, parked on its cushion of air inside the Centre's foyer. There were no exhaust fumes to worry about.

"Hey, magic!" Ryan enthused. "I bet this thing can shift."

"Home first, please," Vicki told the uniformed driver.

It was the smoothest and fastest ride the boys had ever experienced. They would hardly have realized they were moving at all, if the buildings hadn't zipped past at an alarming rate. The view out of the wide windows certainly didn't seem to change very much.

"Not many people about," Dazza observed.

"Perhaps there's something good on the telly!" quipped Anil.

"Do cows and sheep watch TV now as well, then?" put in Jacko. "The fields are empty. Come to mention it, there aren't even many fields."

"Just buildings," added Rakesh. "All looking the same."

"Be better once we get out in the country," said Ryan.

"We should already *be* out in the country," Worm reminded him. "The *Seven Souls* circle was in the middle of moorland."

The hoverbus sighed to a halt in a brightly lit, underground parking area. "This is the Grangelow Village Complex," Tony announced.

"Grangelow?" queried Stopper, the

first word that he had spoken on the journey. His mind was still wrestling with the uncanny coincidence of their shared surname. "This is where my dad was born. He brought us to see the tree and the old well."

"Glad you know about them," said Tony. "They're still here – just."

Vicki turned to the others. "Would you mind waiting a few minutes? We'd like to show Stopper where we live."

"Sure, we'll have a kickabout for a bit," said Ryan.

Vicki checked with the driver. "As long as you don't go outside," she said. "The air quality isn't very good today and rain is forecast."

Ryan shrugged. "OK by me. Never did like getting wet."

"I've noticed," remarked Jacko. "Don't think you've unpacked your soap yet this week!"

"Will you come with me, Worm?"

Stopper asked him. "There's something strange going on here and I'm not sure I can tackle it on my own."

The rest were left to have a game in the deserted, underground parking lot. "Wonder what that's all about with Stopper?" mused Rakesh.

"Search me," said Ryan, blasting the ball at Dazza between the pillars. "Let's just play football. I don't understand anything else round here."

Tony spoke into a voice recognition pad on the wall of the Stoppard apartment and the door slid open. "Welcome home," it greeted them.

The boys glanced suspiciously at the talking door as they entered and then saw Tony press a button by a shelf of what might have been music tapes or videos. They didn't have a chance to investigate. They jumped back as four chairs and a table rose smoothly from the floor.

"Take a seat," Tony invited them. "Vicki's gone to fetch an old family photo you might be interested to see."

Worm groaned to himself. "Oh, wonderful! We travel a hundred and fifty years into the future just to look at their holiday snaps!"

Vicki soon returned with a battered-looking album and placed it carefully on the table in front of them. Worm and Stopper peered at a small, faded photo-graph. It showed a man with his arm wrapped around a boy's shoulders, although the photographer had unfor-tunately chopped off the man's head.

"Incredible!" gasped Worm. "That's you, Stopper."

"Can't be. That's impossible!"

"It's the picture I took at the campsite. Look, there's the side of the minibus – and the stone circle."

Stopper shook his head, as if trying to make better sense of what he was seeing.

"But ... but, I mean, we haven't even had it developed yet..."

"No," Worm frowned. "When it is, your dad's going to be dead narked that I cut his head off."

"How did you come to get this?" Stopper demanded to know, but half-guessed what the answer would be.

Vicki smiled. "It's been passed down through the family," she said proudly. "The boy in the picture became very famous."

"Famous?" Stopper croaked, his mouth suddenly dry.

"Yes, and he's our great-great-great-grandad!"

6 Save the tree

"What's the matter with you?" Jacko asked the white-faced Stopper as they climbed back into the hoverbus. "You look like you've seen a ghost."

"Tell you later," Stopper mumbled. "When I've had a chance to think."

"He's just had a bit of a shock!" grinned Worm.

There were some unpleasant jolts for all the boys during the next hour. The hoverbus sped around the Peak District, presenting them with depressing views of empty reservoirs, dried-up river beds and chopped-down forests.

"Nothing magical about this mystery tour," sighed Anil in dismay.

"Still a mystery, though, why things have become so bad," said Worm.

"I did warn you," Vicki reminded him. "We've got some nice scenery left in places, thanks to the National Park managing to preserve certain areas, but we wanted to show you the worst bits."

"So who's to blame for all this mess?" put in Jacko.

Tony shrugged in response. "Nobody and everybody. It just happened over time before people could do enough to stop it."

"We've heard about the dangers of global warming," said Stopper. "Is this what it's done to the environment?"

Tony nodded. "Atmospheric pollution's increased, and there's also been a few accidents at old nuclear reactors. It's not wise to stay out in the sun or the rain for too long nowadays."

The boys saw what he meant when they returned to Grangelow and stepped outside for the first time. Although the sky was grey and overcast, the air had a different feel, even taste, to it.

"Wouldn't want to be breathing in great lungfuls of this stuff all day," said Dazza, adding a little cough for effect.

"We've deliberately left the tree till last," Vicki said, leading them out of the village complex. "It sums up our problems in a way."

"The Victoria Oak!" gasped Stopper. "Just look at the state it's in!"

"It's sure seen better days," said Rakesh. "Er, like yesterday, for example."

"The well still seems to be working, though," Anil pointed out. "The water's flowing out at a fair rate."

"We're very lucky in this part of the country that we've got good sources of water underground," said Tony. "And the dowsers are always busy searching for more."

"This Oak Tree Well has never run dry, even in the worst of our terrible hot summers," Vicki told them proudly. "We still keep up the tradition of dressing it every year to give thanks for its pure water."

"Dad would have a fit if he saw the poor old tree like this," said Stopper. "It seems to mean a lot to him."

"And to us," stressed Tony. "But it's been so damaged by the pollution that they're planning to cut it down to make way for more buildings. We want to save it."

"Trouble is, it'd cost a lot of money to do all the conservation work on it that's needed," said his sister. "Any ideas?"

"You're asking *us* for advice?" said Jacko in amazement.

"It was your generation that at last took environmental issues seriously," said Tony. "Things would have been far worse today, if you hadn't made various improvements. Even so, accidents happened..."

He checked himself and Vicki apologized. "Sorry, we aren't allowed to give too many details away. If time-guests went back and stopped something from actually happening, it could change the course of history."

"Are you listening to this, Worm?" remarked Ryan pointedly. "Said you shouldn't go around meddling in the past."

"Well, that doesn't stop us fiddling with the future, does it?" Worm grinned. "What's needed here is some kind of publicity stunt to make local people more aware of what's going on."

"And money," added Stopper. "What about doing a sponsored event?"

"What's that? I've never heard of it before," Vicki admitted.

"It's a good easy way of raising funds," Worm explained. "You promise to do something and other people promise to give you money to do it!"

"Sounds like a great idea!" Tony laughed. "But what could we do?"

"How about a sponsored soccer match?" Ryan piped up, flicking the football up on to his head. "Past versus the future!"

"And hold an auction too," Stopper

put in, fired up with enthusiasm.

"What would people like these want to bid for?" asked Anil.

Stopper snatched the ball in mid-air as Ryan tried to show off his juggling skills. "This!" he said in triumph. "Somebody could be the proud owner of a genuine twentieth-century football! Bet they don't make them like they used to!"

Ryan groaned. "Oh, no, not again! Our dads aren't gonna be very pleased if we go and report back without another one."

"All in a good cause," Stopper grinned. "And at least mine would approve – if we ever tried to get him to believe the real reason!"

"Reckon we'll have to think up something better than that," said Ryan.

The Rangers themselves, and Stopper in particular, were soon to find something else very hard to believe. As the hoverbus arrived back at the Centre, they saw the name of the building over the front entrance:

THE KEITH STOPPARD CENTRE FOR ENVIRONMENTAL RESEARCH

7 Goals galore

Thanks to Vicki and Tony's dad, Professor Stoppard, the seven-a-side challenge match was hastily arranged for that very evening in the Centre's indoor arena. The professor also made sure that the local news networks covered the special event, inviting sponsors for the teams and bids for the leather football.

"This fund-raising lark's really caught on," Jacko enthused as the Rangers began to change in the dressing room. "It's just like one of those telethons!"

"The professor told me the bidding's

going wild," grinned Stopper. "I didn't understand the money system he was talking about, but it sounded like a lot."

"And the more goals we score, Tony's team and us, the more money we all raise," said Worm. "We can't lose either way."

"We're not gonna lose at all," Ryan stated flatly. "We want to show these people how football should really be played."

"It's called goalball now, according to Tony," Anil put in. "It's not just played with the feet any more."

"Not sure I understand all the different rules," said Rakesh.

"Don't worry about details," scoffed Ryan. "The game's still about scoring goals – and that's my speciality."

Before the Rangers left the dressing room, Ryan looked at himself in the full-length mirror, admiring the snazzy silver kit they'd been given. "Hey, skipper! D'yer reckon we could wear this in the league next season? Feels great."

"Might not do on cold winter afternoons," Jacko laughed. "It's a bit thin. We'd freeze to death."

There were only a small number of spectators actually in the arena itself to watch the game. But the boys knew that thousands would be viewing their performance from home, supporting the "good cause" by paying to have the action programmed on to their three-dimensional screens.

And the Rangers soon found out that goalball was an all-action game. The arena might have been heated, but the visitors were caught cold by the frenzied start. The rush-hour traffic was nearly all one-way – towards Dazza's hockey-sized goal net. His eyes had lit up when he first saw how small the goals were, but Dazza quickly revised his opinion. Keeping the high-bouncing ball out of them was no easy matter.

"No sweat, man," the goalie had boasted before the kick-off. "I've played plenty of indoor soccer in the school gym. I know all the angles."

Unfortunately, he hadn't taken into account rebounds from the low roof. Captain Tony opened the scoring immediately with an expertly judged, double-handed catch off the ceiling. Dazza was left gaping and flat-footed as the ball was gleefully hurled past him into the net.

"OK, so maybe they play the game a bit differently here," he shrugged, a sickly grin trying to hide his embarrassment.

Goalscoring, future-style, was not exactly a rarity. Goals flew in at both ends almost as often as they do in basketball, mainly because the players were also allowed to handle the ball. Catching and throwing were just as common as kicking.

By the time the Rangers players began to adjust to the new rules, the game had reached the quarter-stage break and they were losing heavily.

"Twelve–five!" snorted Dazza in disgust. "Ridiculous. I don't stand a chance when the shooter can just chuck the ball in with his hands."

"And *hers*!" added Rakesh cheekily. "Vicki's scored at least four!"

"Sasha in their goal seems to be managing all right," Anil remarked. "She's made some great diving stops."

"Huh! She's more used to it, isn't she?" Dazza retorted.

"Well, we've just got to be quick learners," Jacko told his team. "I'll hold back a bit more to support Stopper and Worm in defence. Rakesh, you and Anil be ready to break out fast and help Ryan in attack."

"We ought to have more stamina than

them," Worm calculated. "They can't get as much exercise as we do, being stuck inside more."

"Worm's right," agreed Jacko. "I reckon the longer this game goes on, the more we can get on top as they start to tire. Just got to make sure we're not too far behind by then to catch up."

"And we've got home advantage," Stopper added, smiling at their puzzled faces. "This is my Centre, remember, so this must be my pitch!"

The next period, however, was still controlled by Tony's team. They maintained the same energetic pace, passing the ball around skilfully both on the floor and through the air. They often used neat, clever rebounds to dodge past opponents, too, a vital tactic that the Rangers kept forgetting.

"This is a bit like that old medieval village game – only indoors," Worm panted, leaning briefly on Anil's shoulder. "Anything goes!"

The score mounted up against them as the fifteen-minute quarter raced away, but it was climaxed by an excellent team goal – by the Rangers.

The move started after Dazza pulled off a spectacular save, flinging himself high to the left to clutch the ball just underneath the crossbar. He rolled it out to Worm who linked up well with Jacko and Rakesh down the right flank, enabling the captain to whip the ball across to Ryan in the middle. The Rangers' top striker did the rest. His bullet header was bouncing back out of the net before Sasha could blink.

It was a pure footballing goal that boosted their spirits – as long as they didn't look up at the scoreboard. That showed them trailing 19–9.

"That's the way to play," Jacko urged. "Let's stick to what we know best and prove proper football is better than their new-fangled version."

The second half of the match, as they hoped, began to tell a different story. The Rangers switched the ball about the Astroturf court with growing confidence, making the Future players do a lot of extra chasing. Tony and his teammates were grateful for the short breather before the final period, hanging on now to only a narrow 22-20 lead.

The Rangers were enjoying themselves. Even Worm had scored two goals, both with accurate, long-range skimmers, and he was content to swap places with Dazza to allow the keeper to join in the fun.

Dazza stormed about the court like a mad bull, causing havoc, and the home side were no match for his superior handling skills. He at least felt comfortable catching the ball, and after Jacko notched up the equalizer, it was Dazza who put Rangers in front. With his

head! It was his hat-trick goal, a full-length diving header from Anil's pinpoint pass.

Everybody in the team had scored at least twice, with Ryan claiming a personal tally of ten! By their own reckoning, they seemed to have scored three more than the official total given to them by the umpires, but they were not complaining. Rangers still ran out winners 33–27.

The last word was left to Stopper. He hammered the ball home from the halfway line with stunning power, giving Sasha no hope of keeping it out.

"What a shot!" gasped Vicki as they shook hands afterwards.

Stopper grinned at her. "Yeah, not bad, eh, for a great-great-great-grandad!"

8 Time to go

"What's wrong?" hissed Rakesh.

Worm shrugged. "Dunno. Some kind of technical hitch, I gather."

The seven boys stood anxiously by the stones as the professor's team of scientists reviewed the data on their computer screens.

"We'll get back all right somehow, don't worry," Stopper said, as much to reassure himself as anyone else. "Looks like I've got things to do."

Ryan bounced a ball to relieve his tension. Not their own football, of course, but the one they'd used in the match. It was guaranteed never to puncture. The ball had been given to them as a souvenir, along with the silver strip which they were still wearing under their own clothes.

The Rangers hadn't yet thought up a story to explain away such flashy, futuristic-style kit when they returned, but they were beginning to wonder if they would ever need to. There was only half an hour to go before midnight – their deadline for being transported back on the same time co-ordinates as they left. Vicki and Tony failed to ease their fears.

"We can't yet promise travellers that they'll arrive at precisely the time they want," Vicki confessed.

"Are we talking about being out by minutes – or years?" asked Worm.

"It varies," admitted Tony. "But if the deadline goes by, you'll have to wait till another opportunity comes round."

"And how long might that be?"

"Maybe the same date next year! Anniversaries, remember."

Tony let that fact sink in before he went on. "But at least we could still then set you back more or less at the right time. You might not even have been missed while you were away – if you see what I mean."

They thought about it. "Apart from being a year older," Rakesh pointed out. "Won't that look a bit suspicious?"

"Could be to our advantage, soccer-wise," suggested Ryan mischievously. "We'd be bigger and stronger than others in our league! The opposition would be wanting to check our birth certificates!"

"This time-travel business can get very confusing," said Jacko. "What if we turned up by mistake ten years later? Would we still be like we are – or suddenly become older?"

"Our clothes wouldn't fit us," Rakesh chipped in again.

"Or say we arrived back earlier," wondered Anil. "What'd happen if we met up with ourselves when we were younger?"

"Either way, sounds like a bit embarrassing," said Stopper.

"Come on, look on the bright side," said Worm. "If we *are* stuck in the future for another year, think of all the new things we could learn. All that extra history to study!"

That thought did not exactly cheer everybody else up.

At a quarter to midnight, the five-minute countdown at last began. Each boy was positioned next to one of the ancient stones, in contact with its warm, glowing surface.

"Thanks for saving the Victoria Oak," Tony said to them before he and Vicki had to leave the room. "It's another small victory in the battle for a better environment."

"From little acorns..." Worm murmured. "Every little bit counts."

Vicki smiled at Stopper. "We owe more to you than we're able to say. You'll know what I mean some day. Keep up the good work."

He grinned shyly. "I will. And I'll make sure Dad puts that picture in the family album – as soon as we get it developed!"

The Rangers knew they were taking a calculated risk, but had to put their faith in both ancient and future technology. As the prehistoric stones under their hands grew even warmer and the vibrations increased, they swallowed hard and exchanged nervous grins with each other.

"Last one back home's a cissy!" Dazza called out – and then vanished.

So did the control room. The travellers

felt the same lurch in the pit of their stomachs as before, like going over a humpback bridge in a car too fast. Briefly, they were given a tantalizing glimpse of a group of boys playing football near a stone circle, then there was a jolt and they found themselves standing in a field.

Gingerly, they stepped away from the stones and gazed around, glad there was no one else about to witness their magical reappearance.

"Well, we're back," said Jacko. "And the campsite's over there still."

"Yeah, but we're not even sure what day it is," said Ryan. "Or year!"

"Only one way to find out," said Worm, starting to move off.

They trailed after him towards the site. "Did you lot see what I saw?" said Dazza. "Those kids – I mean us – just before we materialized."

The others nodded. "I recognized you

in goal," Rakesh cackled. "Letting one in as usual!"

"There must have been a final readjustment just in time to prevent us actually overlapping," said Stopper. "We might have been seeing double!"

"Just where did you lot disappear to?" came the loud demand as they approached the tents.

The boys broke into peals of relieved laughter, making Mr Thomas even more annoyed. "The rest came back into camp over an hour ago, saying you went off with those other kids. Typical! Anything to get out of doing the chores here before we leave."

"Sorry, Dad," grinned Ryan. "Time's just flown by this morning."

His dad stood before them, hands on hips, unimpressed. "And what's that ball you've got there? Where's ours?"

"Er, we, um, swapped it for theirs," he stumbled.

"Swapped it!" Mr Thomas cried in disbelief, snatching up the ball. "A brand new leather ball swapped for this thing. It's no more use to us than a beach ball."

He threw the light ball down to the ground in disgust, then watched amazed as it bounced way back up into the air and over the tents. "Go and swap it back this minute."

"Er, that might be a little difficult, Dad. They'll be a long way from here by now."

"Right! We've saved all the clearing-up for your group," he raged. "I don't want to find a single piece of litter left anywhere. Got that?"

The manager was astonished to see how eagerly they all set to work on their tasks, almost as if they really wanted to do it. Ryan not only collected his own can from the hedge, but together with Stopper, cleared the undergrowth of other people's rubbish as well.

Mr Stoppard was equally taken aback. "What's got into you?" he asked his son. "Looks like you'd be prepared to go and tidy the whole site if you had time."

"Wish we could. Any idea where the nearest bottle bank is, Dad?"

"Bottle bank? Have you turned green all of a sudden?"

"Got to think of the future," he said seriously. "Recycling is very important. Everybody should try and do their bit for the environment."

Mr Stoppard shook his head. "But you've never bothered about such stuff before."

"Never too late to start. Think I might even go into this line of work when I grow up! You know, conservation and all that."

"A wise decision that, Grandad, I'd say," chuckled Worm as he walked past with handfuls of litter for the black bag.

"Grandad! Why on earth should he call you that?"

Stopper thought quickly for an answer. "Not sure. Er, maybe he's just worked out I'm the oldest member of the squad. You know what Worm's like for dates, Dad."

After their tents had been loaded into the minibuses, the boys double-checked to make certain that no rubbish of any kind had been left behind. The Rangers were on their way to spend the last night of the Easter tour in a hostel, in proper beds – but not before the long walk that had been threatened.

There were not even any of the expected protests about that. "Looking forward to breathing in all that lovely clean, fresh air up on the hills," said Jacko. "How about you, gang?"

"Sure thing," Dazza agreed. "Can't beat it. Let's make the most of it while we can."

"Great. So will we," laughed Mr Stoppard. "Makes a nice change to have nobody moaning about clearing up or going for a walk."

"C'mon, then," said Mr Thomas. "Got to press on, we're late setting off already. We're up against the clock, I'm afraid."

"It'll always be a race against time," said Stopper to himself. "But at least I know which course to take now. It's green for go!"

TIME RANGERS

The time tour continues with:

4. A Ghost of a Chance

Worm and Anil passed the ball between them a few times while the mill children watched the demonstration in obedient silence. Ryan, however, soon lost his patience.

The Rangers' top striker stepped in to intercept a pass and dribbled the ball away before lashing it against a wall. "GOAL!" he yelled at the top of his voice, punching the air in mock celebration. "GOAL!"

All the children laughed and Whizzer was the first to react. He ran after the rebound, controlled the awkward bounce with remarkable ease and then copied Ryan's shot. The ball flew into the wall not as powerfully as Ryan's effort but almost in the same place, just missing a girl's head.

"GOAL!" he squealed, imitating Ryan's antics by jumping up and down and waving his fists about. "GOAL!"